Rabbit & Robot

The Sleepover

Rabbit & Robot
The Sleepover

Cece Bell

CANDLEWICK PRESS

For my mama, Barbara Bell,
the best list maker in the world

First edition 2012

Library of Congress Catalog Card Number 2011048365
ISBN 978-0-7636-5475-7

13 14 15 16 17 WOR 10 9 8 7 6 5 4

Printed in Stevens Point, WI, U.S.A.

This book was typeset in Scala and Digital.
The illustrations were created digitally.

Candlewick Press
99 Dover Street
Somerville, Massachusetts 02144

visit us at www.candlewick.com

CONTENTS

CHAPTER ONE
Make Pizza

Rabbit was excited. His friend Robot was coming to spend the night. Rabbit had everything planned out.

Ding dong!

Rabbit opened the door.

"Hi, Robot," said Rabbit. "I am so happy you are here."

"Greetings, Rabbit," said Robot. "Thank you for inviting me."

"You're welcome," said Rabbit. "Now, I have made a list of the things we will do."

1. Make pizza
2. Watch TV
3. Play Go Fish
4. Go to bed

"Can we play Old Maid, too?" asked Robot. "I think the Old Maid is cute."

"Old Maid is *not* on the list," said Rabbit.

"How about Crazy Eights? I am crazy about Crazy Eights."

"No way," said Rabbit. "Crazy Eights is not on the list, either."

"I see," said Robot.

"So," said Rabbit, "first on the list is
to make pizza."

"Good," said Robot. "My Built-in
Food-o-Meter reports that I am hungry.
I must eat."

Rabbit got two frozen pizzas out of
the freezer.

"Cheese pizza," said Rabbit. "I have carrots and lettuce and snow peas to put on top of the pizzas. I am going to put all three on my pizza."

"Oh," said Robot.

"What is the matter?" asked Rabbit.

"Don't you like carrots?"

"I do not," answered Robot.

"Do you like lettuce?" asked Rabbit.

"I do not," said Robot.

"Snow peas?"

"Ouch," cried Rabbit. "That hurt!
Turn down your Volume Knob!"

"I apologize," said Robot.

"What do *you* put on *your* pizza?" asked Rabbit.

"Hardware," answered Robot. "Nuts and bolts and screws."

"Yuck!" said Rabbit. "I do not have any nuts or bolts or screws. Sorry."

"That's OK," said Robot. "My Magnetic Hands will find some." Robot rolled through Rabbit's house. He waved his Magnetic Hands up and down and all around.

"Eureka!" Robot yelled. "Your table and chairs are held together with nuts and bolts and screws!"

Robot lifted a flap on his side. He took out his tool-box and found a wrench and a screwdriver.

Robot used the wrench to take the
nuts and bolts out of the table.

He used the screwdriver to take the
screws out of the chairs.

"My table!" howled Rabbit. "My chairs!"

"Do not be alarmed," said Robot.

But Rabbit *was* alarmed. "We were supposed to eat our pizzas sitting at the table," he said. "Now what?"

Rabbit started
yelling. "Where
are we going to
eat?" he cried.
He yelled all
around the house.

He started throwing things, too.

Robot prepared the pizzas. He put
the nuts and bolts and screws on his
pizza. He put the carrots and lettuce
and snow peas on Rabbit's pizza. He
put both pizzas in
the oven.

Rabbit was still yelling. He was still throwing things.

Robot turned up his Volume Knob. "I can solve our problem!" he shouted.

Rabbit stopped yelling. He stopped throwing things. "Oh, yeah?" he said. "How?"

"Do you have a blanket?" asked Robot.

"I do," said Rabbit. "But it is not time for bed. That is Number Four on the list."

"The blanket is not for sleeping,"
said Robot.

Rabbit gave Robot a blanket. Robot
spread the blanket on the floor.

"Sit down, Rabbit," he said.

Rabbit sat down.

Robot got the pizzas out of the oven. He brought them to Rabbit on the blanket.

"Picnic!" said Robot.

"Oh, picnic," said Rabbit. He bit into his pizza.

"My Built-in Food-o-Meter approves of this pizza," said Robot.

"Yes, this picnic is pretty fun," said Rabbit. "I'll cross 'Make Pizza' off the list, even though you put weird things on yours."

"Thank you, Rabbit," said Robot.

CHAPTER TWO
WATCH TV

"Next on the list is to watch TV," said Rabbit. "My favorite show is coming on soon. It is called *Cowboy Jack Rabbit.* I do not want to miss it."

"I like TV," said Robot.

"Everything is ready," said Rabbit. "I have dusted the TV. I have plumped the sofa cushions. I have popped the popcorn. All I need is the TV remote."

Rabbit went to the TV to get the remote.

"Oh, no," moaned Rabbit. "The remote is not here. I always leave the remote on top of the TV."

"Do not panic," said Robot.

Rabbit panicked. He checked the top of the TV again. "It is definitely not on top of the TV," he said.

"I have some data that will interest you," said Robot.

Rabbit looked under the sofa cushions. "It is not under the sofa cushions," he cried.

"There is a logical solution to your problem," said Robot.

Rabbit dumped the popcorn out of the bowl. "It is not in the popcorn!" he shouted.

"BEEP! BEEP! BEEP!" beeped Robot.

"Don't you beep at me!" hollered Rabbit. "If we don't find the remote, we will never see *Cowboy Jack Rabbit* ever again. We will never see *any* TV ever again!"

Rabbit ran around the house, yelling.

Rabbit stopped running. He stopped yelling.

"I have some data that will interest you," said Robot. "Follow me."

Robot led Rabbit to the bathroom.
He pointed to the mirror.

"Observe your reflection," said
Robot.

Rabbit looked in the mirror.

He found the remote. "Aw, gee, Robot," said Rabbit. "Why didn't you just tell me?"

CHAPTER THREE
Play Go Fish

Rabbit turned off the TV. "What a fantastic show," he said. "And now it is time for Number Three on the list: Play Go Fish."

"Oooooooh Kaaaaaaay," mumbled Robot.

Rabbit and Robot sat down on the
blanket. Rabbit dealt the cards and
began the game.

"Give me all your tens," said Rabbit.

Robot said nothing.

"Robot!" shouted Rabbit. "I said,
Give me all your tens!"

Robot twitched. "I apologize, Rabbit. I am tired."

"Tired?" said Rabbit. "But we have not checked 'Play Go Fish' off the list. It is not time for bed."

Robot lay down on the blanket. He closed his metal eyelids. His gears began to grind.

"Humm," snored Robot.

"What am I going to do now?" wailed Rabbit. "A nap before bedtime is not on the list. And I was winning that game! Wake up, Robot!"

A narrow strip of paper came out
of a small slot on Robot's front. There
were letters on it:

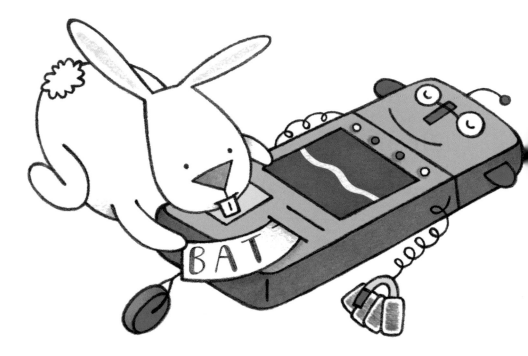

"BAT?" said Rabbit. "Maybe Robot
is trying to tell me something. Maybe I
need to scare Robot to wake him up."

Rabbit ran to his toy chest and found a rubber bat. It had wings and fangs and tiny feet.

"This bat would scare anybody," said Rabbit. He showed the bat to the sleeping Robot.

"Hummmm," snored Robot.

"That did not work," said Rabbit. "Maybe I need a baseball bat. Maybe I need to hit Robot to wake him up."

Rabbit ran back to his toy chest and found a baseball bat. He lifted the baseball bat over his head. "I hope I do not hurt him," he said.

But then more letters appeared on the narrow strip of paper:

"Batter?" cried Rabbit. "Will batter help Robot wake up? Making batter is not on the list, either. But maybe it will work."

Rabbit went to his kitchen. He found a recipe for cake batter in a cookbook. Rabbit beat butter and sugar and eggs and flour with an electric mixer. The batter tasted delicious.

"Robot," said Rabbit, "I know you eat metal stuff. But here is some yummy batter for you."

"Hummmmmm," snored Robot.

"Wake up already!" shouted Rabbit. "We can play Old Maid, too, if you would just WAKE UP!"

Just then, even more letters appeared on the narrow strip of paper:

"Oh!" said Rabbit. "His batteries ran down!" Rabbit opened Robot and took out Robot's old batteries. Then he opened the TV remote and took out the remote's new batteries. Rabbit put the new batteries inside Robot. Robot began to twitch. And then —

"Gee whiz!" cried Rabbit. "Turn down your Volume Knob!"

"Oh," said Robot. "I apologize."

"And where is my thank-you?" asked Rabbit.

"Thank you for the batteries," whispered Robot.

"You're welcome," said Rabbit.

"Let's play Old Maid next!" yelled Robot.

"Good grief," said Rabbit.

CHAPTER FOUR
Go to Bed

Rabbit yawned. "Twenty games is too many," he said. "I am ready for the last thing on the list: Go to bed."

"I am one hundred percent alert," said Robot. "The batteries you gave me are excellent. And I do love Old Maid. But I will come to bed also."

Rabbit brushed his teeth.

Robot polished the metal in his mouth.

Rabbit put on his pajamas. "Where are your pajamas, Robot?" he asked. "You are supposed to bring pajamas to a sleepover."

"I forgot," said Robot with a shrug.

"Oh, dear," said Rabbit. "Here. You can borrow a pair of mine."

Robot put on Rabbit's pajamas.

Rabbit giggled.

"What is so humorous?" asked

Robot.

Rabbit led Robot to the bathroom.

He pointed to the mirror and said,

"Observe your reflection."

Robot looked in the mirror. He smiled. "That *is* humorous," he agreed.

Rabbit got in one bed. Robot got in the other bed.

"Lights out," said Rabbit. He turned off the light. "Good night, Robot."

Rabbit closed his eyes. He began to snore. Robot did not close his eyes. He began to talk.

"Rabbit," said Robot, "I have
reviewed today's data."

"That's nice," said Rabbit. "But the
list says that it is time to sleep. It is not
time to talk. Good night, Robot."

"Rabbit?"

"What?"

"I have reviewed today's data."

"Yes, I know!" hollered Rabbit. "Go
to sleep, Robot."

Robot kept talking. "Just for you, I have organized today's data into a list. My list shows that we did many fun things:

1. WE ENJOYED A PIZZA PICNIC.
2. WE LAUGHED ABOUT THE TV REMOTE IN YOUR EAR.
3. WE PLAYED GO FISH AND OLD MAID.
4. WE GIGGLED WHEN I PUT ON YOUR PAJAMAS.

I have reviewed today's data and the result is: Today was a good day."

"Yes," agreed Rabbit. "It was a good day. Maybe tomorrow, you can make our list of things to do."

"Really?" asked Robot.

"I said *maybe*," answered Rabbit.

"Good night, Robot."

"Good night, Rabbit."